Welcome to The GROW & READ Early Reader Program!

The GROW & READ book program was developed under the supervision of reading specialists to develop kids' reading skills while emphasizing the delight of storytelling. The series was created to help children enjoy learning to read and is perfect for shared reading and reading aloud.

These GROW & READ levels will help you choose the best book for every reader.

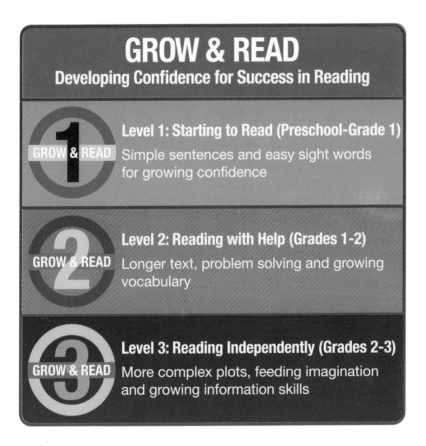

GROW & READ
Developing Confidence for Success in Reading

Level 1: Starting to Read (Preschool-Grade 1)
Simple sentences and easy sight words for growing confidence

Level 2: Reading with Help (Grades 1-2)
Longer text, problem solving and growing vocabulary

Level 3: Reading Independently (Grades 2-3)
More complex plots, feeding imagination and growing information skills

For more information visit growandread.com.

Published by Fabled Films LLC, New York

ISBN: 978-1-944020-15-6

Library of Congress Control Number: 2017936587

Second Edition: November 2017

3 5 7 9 10 8 6 4 2

Cover Designed by Jaime Mendola-Hobbie
Jacket Art by Waymond Singleton
Interior Book Design by Aleks Gulan
Typeset in Helvetica Neue, Mrs. Ant, Pacific Northwest, and Stemple Garamond
Printed by Everbest in China

FABLED FILMS PRESS
NEW YORK CITY
fabledfilms.com

For information on bulk purchases for promotional use please contact Consortium Book Sales & Distribution Sales department at ingrampublishersvcs@ingramcontent.com or 1-866-400-5351.

The
Moonlight Meeting

by

Tracey Hecht
& Rumur Dowling

Illustrations by
Waymond Singleton

Fabled Films Press
New York

Chapter 1

The sun had set.

The first stars had begun to shine.

It was nighttime.

But one small, scaly animal was just waking up.

It was Tobin.

Tobin was a pangolin.

"Oh my," Tobin said.

"I smell something delicious!"

Tobin yawned and
stretched his sleepy body.

Tobin sniffed the air
with his long, pointy snout.

Tobin smiled at the big,
bright moon.

Tobin was hungry.

Tobin toddled through the moonlit grass.

Tobin sniffed the cool, wet ground.

"Oof!"

Tobin's snout bonked into something round and soft.

"Oh goodness," Tobin said.

"This is what smells so good.

A pomelo!"

Tobin reached for the greenish-gold fruit.

Suddenly, a voice screeched from above.

"Thief!" it cried.

The voice was coming from the tree.

Tobin was not alone.

Chapter 2

Tobin looked up at the tree.

A small, furry creature stared back at him.

It had big, brown eyes.

It had silver, stretchy wings.

"Oh my!" Tobin cried.

Tobin trembled.

Tobin dropped the pomelo.

Tobin let out a stinky poof!

"*PEE-YEW!*" cried the creature
in the tree.

The small animal pinched
its nose.

"That STENCH!

That ODOR!

That TANG!"

"This calls for the flaps!"

The small animal flapped
its wings.

The small animal
jumped from the tree.

The small animal landed
right in front of Tobin.

Tobin was scared of the small animal.

But he was also curious.

Tobin wanted a friend.

Could this small animal be a friend?

Chapter 3

"Listen up, thief," the small animal said.

"That is my pomelo.

I saw it first."

The small animal put

his hands on his hips.

The small animal tapped

his little foot.

This animal was small, but his

personality was big.

"Oh goodness, a thief?" Tobin asked.

He scratched his scaly head.

Was he a thief?

Tobin did not feel like a thief.

"Yes, you are a thief," the small animal said.

"A pomelo-stealing thief.
And what am I, you might wonder?"

the small animal asked.

"I am Bismark!
Sugar glider spec-tac- u-lar!
And the owner of this pomelo."

Bismark put both hands on the fruit.

"But...I'm not a—"

Tobin started to speak.

Behind them the bushes rustled.

Tobin and Bismark turned their heads.

Someone was coming!

Chapter 4

"Excuse me," said a voice from the bushes.

A sleek fox stepped from the brush.

The fox twitched her nose.

"Do I smell a problem?" the fox asked.

She had detected Tobin's stinky spray.

"Oh goodness," Tobin said.

Tobin bowed his head.

"That was me. I spray when I am scared—and it stinks."

Tobin felt embarrassed.

First he was a thief,

and now he was stinky, too!

But the fox did not pinch her nose.

The fox did not try to wave the

stink away.

Instead, the fox smiled.

She had kind eyes.

She had a warm smile.

Tobin felt much better.

Chapter 5

"Eh-hem!"

Bismark cleared his throat.

"Well, actually, " he piped up.

"There is a problem."

Bismark pointed to Tobin.

"This pangolin was stealing my pomelo!

He is a thief!"

The fox looked at Bismark.

The fox looked at Tobin.

"Is this true?"
the fox asked Tobin.

"Oh goodness..." Tobin said.

Tobin took a deep breath.

Tobin was shy, but this fox

made him feel brave.

"No, I am not a thief," Tobin said.

Bismark raised his tiny fist
to the night sky.

"Incorrecto. Falso!" Bismark said.

"This pomelo does not belong to
this pangolin!

I saw it first."

The fox considered the problem.

There was one pomelo.

There were two of them.

She made a decision.

She raised a sharp claw.

The fox's sharp claw glinted in

the moonlight.

"There is only one thing to do,"

the fox said.

Bismark gasped.

Tobin gulped!

Chapter 6

The fox sliced the pomelo with her claw.

The fox sliced again.

The fox smiled her warm smile.

"Why don't we share?" she said.

"Phew!" Tobin sighed.

"Ooh la la!" Bismark chimed in.

This fox was in charge.

The fox pushed a piece of pomelo to Tobin.

She pushed a piece of pomelo to Bismark.

She took a piece for herself.

"Mmm," Tobin said.

The pomelo was sweet!

"Burp," Bismark belched.

The pomelo was juicy.

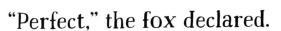

"Perfect," the fox declared.

The pomelo was delicious!

41

Chapter 7

Bismark finished his fruit.

He winked at Tobin.

He turned to the fox.

"Mi bella—" Bismark began.

Bismark licked his paw.

He used it to smooth a hair across
his bald spot.

"Allow me to introduce us,"
Bismark said to the fox.

"The pangolin is Tobin."

Bismark cleared his throat.

"And I—" Bismark made a grand swoop
with his arm.

"I am Bismark!

Sugar glider spec-tac-u-lar!"

The fox looked down at the silly
sugar glider.

She could not help herself.

Her mouth curled into a gentle smile.

"I am Dawn," she said.

Bismark took a small leap.

"Dawn?" he said.

"Dawn? The time of day the sun comes up!

The time of day I go to sleep!

The time of day I dream!"

Bismark took to one knee.

"Of course! Mi bella. Dawn.

I will call you, Fox of My Dreams!"

Tobin giggled.

But then he paused.

"Oh goodness!" he exclaimed.

Tobin suddenly realized

something very important.

Chapter 8

"Bismark, do you also sleep during the day?" Tobin asked.

"Si, si!" Bismark replied.

He hopped to his feet.

"I am a night prowler.

I find my bugs and berries when the moon is bright.

And you, Fox of My Dreams?" Bismark asked Dawn.

"Do you sleep during the day?"

Dawn swished her white tipped tail.

"I do," she replied.

Tobin clapped his long, taloned paws.

"We're all nocturnal!" Tobin said.

"Awake by night, asleep by day!"

"By the stars!" Bismark cried.

"We will be a moonlight trio!

We will be a nocturnal brigade!

We will be—"

"We will be friends," Dawn finished.

Tobin looked to the left.

He saw a small and spunky sugar glider.

Tobin looked to the right.

He saw a strong and serious fox.

Tobin looked up at the moon.

His eyes sparkled.

Friends.

They would be friends.

The NoCTURNALS

FUN FACTS!

What are The Nocturnal Animals?

Pangolin: The pangolin is covered with keratin scales on most of its body except its belly and face. Pangolins spray a stinky odor, much like a skunk, to ward off danger. It then curls into a ball to protect against attack. Pangolins have long, sticky tongues to eat ants and termites. Pangolins do not have teeth.

Red Fox: The red fox has reddish fur with a big bushy tail and a white tip. Red foxes are clever creatures with keen eyesight. They have large, upright ears to hear sounds far away.

Sugar Glider: The sugar glider is a small marsupial. It looks like a flying squirrel. It has short, gray fur and black rings around its big eyes. It has a black stripe that runs from its nose to the end of its tail. Sugar gliders have special skin that stretches from the ankle to the wrist. This special skin allows sugar gliders to glide from tree to tree to find food and escape danger.

Nighttime Fun Facts!

Nocturnal animals are animals that are awake and active at night. They sleep during the day.

Pomelos are fruits much like grapefruits. They have yellow or light green peels and pink citrusy flesh. They are the biggest citrus fruits in the world!

N(The)CTURNALS

Look for The Next Adventure!

Join The Nocturnal Brigade at nocturnalsworld.com for updates!

Welcome to The GROW & READ Early Reader Program!

The GROW & READ book program was developed under the supervision of reading specialists to develop kids' reading skills while emphasizing the delight of storytelling.

To compliment the narrative, each book has illustrations that strengthen the understanding of the story.

The series can help children enjoy learning to read and is perfect for shared reading and reading aloud.

Visit growandread.com to download the educational materials we have created for teachers and librarians.

#NocturnalsWorld

About the Authors

Tracey Hecht is a writer and entrepreneur who has written, directed and produced for film. She has created a Nocturnals Read Aloud Writing program for middle graders in partnership with the New York Public Library that has expanded nationwide. She splits her time between Oquossoc, Maine and New York City.

Rumur Dowling is a writer for Fabled Films Press. He studied English and creative writing at Harvard University and eighteenth-century poetry at Oxford as a Henry Fellow. He now lives in his hometown of New York City. This is his first children's book.

About the Illustrator

Waymond Singleton is an illustrator and animator. He received his BFA in Animation from Savannah College of Art and Design. He grew up in Beaufort, South Carolina and now lives in Brooklyn, where he spends his free time making short films. This is his first children's book.

About Fabled Films

Fabled Films is a publishing and entertainment company creating original content for middle grade and Y/A audiences. Fabled Films Press combines strong literary properties with high quality production values to connect books with generations of parents and their children. Each property is supported with additional content in the form of animated web series and social media as well as websites featuring activities for children, parents, bookstores, educators and librarians.

FABLED FILMS PRESS
NEW YORK CITY
fabledfilms.com

Read All Three Nocturnal Adventures!

"The characters are delightful and the nighttime landscape is captivating."—R.L. Stine

Visit nocturnalsworld.com to
watch animated videos, download fun nighttime
activities, listen to author Tracey Hecht read the books aloud,
and view a map of the Brigade's adventure at
www.nocturnalsworld.com/map/.

Teachers and librarians get Common Core Language Arts and
Next Generation Science guides for the book series.

www.nocturnalsworld.com
#NocturnalsWorld